W9-BNK-422

Ralph Troll's New Bicycle

A Norfin® Troll Tale

Illustrated by Jill Dubin
by Nancy E. Krulik

No part of this publication may be reproduced in whole or in part, or stored in a retrieval system, or transmitted in any form or by any means, electronic, mechanical, photocopying, recording, or otherwise, without written permission of the publisher. For information regarding permission, write to EFS Marketing Associates, Inc., 164 Central Avenue, Farmingdale, NY 11735.

ISBN 0-590-45924-4

Copyright © 1992 by The Troll Company, Aps.
All rights reserved. Published by Scholastic Inc.,
730 Broadway, New York, NY 10003, by arrangement with
EFS Marketing Associates, Inc.
NORFIN is a registered trademark of EFS Marketing Associates, Inc.

12 11 10 9 8 7 6 5 4 3 2 1   2 3 4 5 6 7/9

Printed in the U.S.A.

First Scholastic printing, September 1992

SCHOLASTIC INC.

New York Toronto London Auckland Sydney

Ralph Troll was very proud of his first bicycle. It had a big silver horn that toot-toot-tooted whenever he squeezed its black rubber bulb. On the handlebars sat a red-and-white wicker basket just the right size for carrying fresh blueberries home to his mother. Best of all, the bike was bright red — Ralph's favorite color. The only thing wrong with Ralph's new bicycle was that it had training wheels.

"Now that I have my own bicycle, can I go on a bike hike with you and your friends?" Ralph asked his big sister, Erika.

"No, you may not!" Erika said angrily. "I am tired of having you tag along with me. Besides, we are going on a long bike hike — over the hills and through the forest. You couldn't possibly keep up with us on your little kid bike with training wheels. Why don't you stay here and play with your rock collection?"

Ralph started to cry. It just wasn't fair!

He watched sadly as Erika and her friends, Henry, Casey, and Greta, rode off into the hills. He really wanted to go with them. And he was sure his new red bicycle could keep up — even with training wheels!

"I'll show them!" Ralph shouted. "I can *too* keep up with the big trolls!"

And with that, Ralph shoved his rocks into his backpack so fast that he didn't even notice that he left the flap open. He quickly hopped on his bike, and rode off into the hills.

Going uphill wasn't easy. Ralph pedaled as hard as he could. He looked straight ahead, keeping his sister and her friends in sight. But he made sure to stay a few feet behind them. Ralph had to be very careful that Erika didn't see him. If she did, she was sure to send him home!

Ralph was so busy looking at his sister, he didn't even notice that rocks were falling out of his backpack, one by one.

The sun was high in the sky. It was getting very warm. Ralph followed his sister and her friends as they rode through the forest, past beautiful yellow wildflowers and around brand-new pine tree saplings. Ralph was very hot and very tired and he wished he could rest. But Ralph kept on pedaling.

"I can keep going as long as they can!" he said defiantly.

Erika, Henry, Casey, and Greta finally
stopped pedaling. They parked their bikes by
a bunch of wild lilies and sat down on the
bank of a cool, clear stream.

Ralph rested under a giant wild mushroom,
a few feet away from them.

"Time for a picnic!" Greta smiled as she
pulled a tuna fish sandwich from her
backpack.

Ralph watched silently as Erika removed
a blue-and-white checkered blanket from
her backpack. His mouth watered as she
unwrapped a thick hunk of cheese and one
of the fresh rolls their mother had baked
that morning.

Grrr! Ralph's stomach grumbled with hunger. He would have liked a piece of that cheese for himself. And his throat was awfully dry. Some of Casey's cool, wet apple cider would certainly have felt good going down.

But Ralph didn't say a word. He sat quietly in his hiding place.

"Boy, am I hot!" Henry said. "Let's go for a swim!"

One by one, the bigger trolls pulled off their T-shirts. They were wearing bathing suits underneath.

"Last one in is a rotten egg!" Erika called as she dove into the cool, clear water.

Ralph wiped the sweat from his forehead. Ralph was so hot, he almost forgot he was supposed to be hiding. He started to walk toward the stream. Just as Erika turned in his direction, Ralph dove behind a dandelion and hid under its golden yellow petals.

"Whew, that was close!" he whispered to his new red bicycle.

The bigger trolls splashed in the water all
that day. Ralph got tired of watching them.
He curled up in the green grass and took a
nap.

When Ralph woke up, the sun was starting
to set. Erika and her friends were putting on
their T-shirts and getting ready to bike home.

"This was a great day." Erika smiled. "Just
me and my best friends. No baby brother to
watch out for."

That made Ralph mad! He had never asked
his sister to watch out for him! All he had
ever asked her to do was to play with him!

Ralph slipped his backpack onto his back.
It felt lighter than before. Ralph reached back
and felt inside his pack. Oh no! His rock
collection had disappeared.

"Darn!" Ralph muttered. "Not only did I
have a rotten day, but now I've lost my rock
collection, too!"

The sun was setting quickly now. It was getting close to suppertime! Ralph wished his sister would hurry up and leave so he could follow her home.

"Follow me down the mountain," Erika
called to Greta, Henry, and Casey.

"We don't go down that mountain," Henry
said. "We ride past that tree and down the
road."

"No, we don't," Greta answered. "We follow
the stream back to town."

Casey started to cry. "Oh, no! We're lost.
We'll be stuck out here forever!"

Ralph got scared. Soon it would be dark. He could hear the hoot of the owls and the hiss of the night animals as they scurried from tree to tree.

Crack! Ralph heard a twig break behind him when a mouse rushed by. He turned in the direction of the noise. Ralph's eyes opened wide. There, before him, was a path of beautifully colored stones.

His rock collection! The rocks had fallen out of Ralph's backpack and made a path toward home!

Ralph was so excited, he forgot he was supposed to be hiding from his big sister.

"Erika, Erika!" Ralph called out from behind the trees. "I can get us home!"

Erika turned to look at Ralph. "Ralph, what are you doing here? I told you to stay at home."

Greta pulled at her friend's arm. "If Ralph can help us get home, then it's a good thing he's here!" she said.

Ralph was very proud of himself. "Just follow me," he told the bigger trolls. "I'll lead you right to my house."

And that's just what he did.

When Ralph and Erika reached the front
door of their house, Erika whispered in
Ralph's ear. "If you promise not to tell Mama
we got lost, I promise to teach you to ride
your bike without training wheels!"

Ralph smiled. "It's a deal!"

The next morning, true to her word, Erika used her father's tools to take the training wheels off Ralph's bicycle. She showed him how to balance himself on just two wheels. She held on to the back of the bike and ran, while Ralph pedaled.

"Okay, Erika, let go!" Ralph called out to his sister. "I can do it myself now!"

And off he went!

The very next day, Erika, Casey, Henry, and Greta went on another bike hike. This time, it was Ralph who led the way on his very own two-wheeler!